THIS CANDLEWICK BOOK BELONGS TO:

_____

_____

_____

_____

For the new gang —
Micha, Amira, Tristan,
Clarke, Matthew, and Monica ~ J. H.

For Max ~ **B. G.**

Eyes, Nose

Text copyright © 1999 by Judy Hindley
Illustrations copyright © 1999 by Brita Granström

First U.S. paperback edition 2002

The Library of Congress has cataloged the hardcover edition as follows:

Hindley, Judy.
Eyes, nose, fingers, and toes : a first book about you / by Judy Hindley ;
illustrated by Brita Granström. —1st U.S. ed.
p.   cm.
Summary: A group of toddlers demonstrate all the fun things
that they can do with their eyes, ears, mouths, hands, legs, feet—
and everything in between.
ISBN 978-0-7636-0440-0 (hardcover)
[1. Body, Human—Fiction. 2. Toddlers—Fiction. 3. Stories in rhyme.]
I. Granström, Brita, ill. II. Title.
PZ8.3.H5555Ki   1998
[E]—dc21   98-23597
ISBN 978-0-7636-1708-0 (paperback)

09 10 11 12 13 WKT 15 14 13 12 11 10
Printed in Shenzhen, Guangdong,China

This book was typeset in Gararond.
The illustrations were done in pencil, watercolor, and crayon.

Candlewick Press
99 Dover Street
Somerville,MA 02144
visit us at www.candlewick.com

ingers, and Toes

A First Book All About You

Judy Hindley

illustrated by
Brita Granström

CANDLEWICK PRESS

Eyes are to blink, eyes are to wink.
Eyes are for looking and finding—**You!**
Eyes are to shut when you're asleep.
Eyes are for hiding . . .

A nose is to blow.
A nose is to sniff.
A nose has holes
for sniffing with.

Ears are to find at
the sides of your head.
Are you wearing your
ears today?
Hurray!
Ears are to hear
a story with.

A mouth is to yawn . . .
Open
wide—
See all the teeth
and the tongue
inside?

A mouth is to laugh—

Ha-ha! Ha-ha!

A tongue is to talk
and to sing—La-la!

La-la,

la-la,

la-la!

Lips are to make

very small

for a kiss.

Lips are to whistle
and blow.

ps are to stretch

very wide for a smile,

and round

when your mouth

goes—

Ho!

Ho!

Ho!

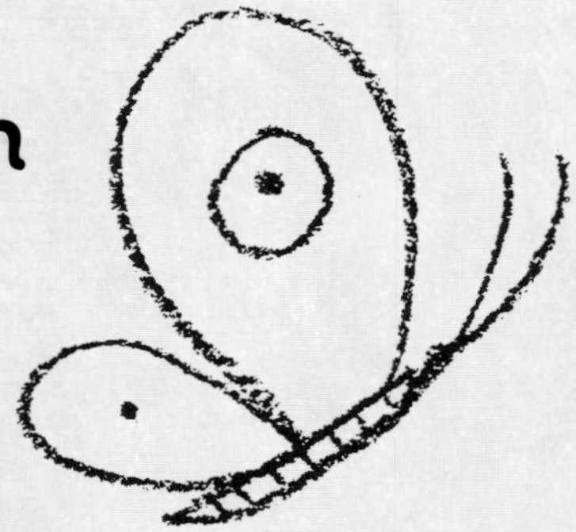

Feel how it makes

your belly go

when you laugh—

Ha-ha!

Hee-hee!

Ho-

ho!

What about necks?
A neck is to tickle.
What about shoulders?
Those are to wriggle.

A back
is to
stretch
so high
and
tall.

A back is
to curl up
snug
and small.

Arms go up,

Arms go down.

Arms go
reaching way
out wide.
Arms can
rock you
side to
side.

Hands
are to hold
and pat

and
clap!

Hands are to
hide
behind your
back.

Fingers and thumbs
are for counting on—
One,
two, three,
four,
five . . .

and then,

six, seven, eight,
nine, ten.

Let's find some toes
and count up those—
and then
let's wiggle
and
waggle each one!

Legs are
for
leaping
and
jumping
and dancing.

and skipping
and hopping.

Legs are
for kicking

Feet are for STOMPING and suddenly—

STOPPING!

Knees are to bend,
so let's all sit down—

BUMP!

On our bottoms,
side by side.

So here we are!
And I'll tell you again—
Kisses are little

miles are wide—

A hug is a bundle
with YOU
inside.

JUDY HINDLEY says *Eyes, Nose, Fingers, and Toes: A First Book All About You*
"is a book to play with. I hope it encourages children to express and celebrate
the sheer delight of owning a body." She is the author of many other children's
books, including *A Song of Colors, One By One, The Best Thing About a Puppy,
The Big Red Bus,* and *The Perfect Little Monster.*

BRITA GRANSTRÖM, who has illustrated more than twenty-five children's books,
says of *Eyes, Nose, Fingers, and Toes: A First Book All About You,* "It has
been great fun—and it's drawn from my heart. I hope it shows."